THE GREAT RED FUZZY

By Dauna Howe

Illustrated by the Author

Archway Publishing books may be ordered through booksellers or by contacting:

Archway Publishing
1663 Liberty Drive
Bloomington, IN 47403
www.archwaypublishing.com
1-(888)-242-5904

Because of the dynamic nature of the Internet, any web addresses or links contained in this book may have changed since publication and may no longer be valid. The views expressed in this work are solely those of the author and do not necessarily reflect the views of the publisher, and the publisher hereby disclaims any responsibility for them.

Any people depicted in stock imagery provided by Thinkstock are models, and such images are being used for illustrative purposes only.

Certain stock imagery © Thinkstock.

ISBN: 978-1-4808-0505-7 (sc)
ISBN: 978-1-4808-0508-8 (e)

Printed in the United States of America

Archway Publishing rev. date: 04/30/14

The Great Red Fuzzy came to town

And on its face was a terrible frown.

"Make way! Make way!"
it was heard to say.
**"I'm the Great Red Fuzzy,
and I'm here to stay!"**

It had two long legs which
made it quite tall,
And one blinking black eye that
looked round like a ball.
Its green nose was short, and
shaped like a carrot,
With a wide mouth below that
snapped like a parrot's.

It stomped all around, both
this way and that
Til it found a big rock upon which it sat.
Three frightened dogs ran,
both that way and this,
While five children hid, and
a cat went, "Hiss!"

"I am so thirsty I could drink
A whole sea!
I need some cold water!
Show it to me!"

The Great Red Fuzzy then
hopped right down.
He saw a small stream that
ran right through town.
And he drank it all up with
a slurping sound.

"I'm sleepy now! My brain needs a rest!
"I need a big bed, one
that's soft like a nest!"

The people ran quickly all over the place,
And brought their own pillows
to fill a large space.
While the Great Red Fuzzy took a long nap,
The people all gathered to think of a trap.

The people all whispered,
"Shall we get a big net?
"Should we use a big hose
and get it all wet?
"Oh dear, oh dear! What can we do?"
And the Great Red Fuzzy yelled,
"I can hear you!"

It looked all around with its one scary eye
Until it saw something that
looked like a pie.
"What's that?" it demanded.
"I like what I see!
"Bring it at once! Bring it to me!
"Bring me some food, and
bring it here soon!
"I'm hungry enough to
eat the new moon!"

The people ran forth. The people ran back.
They brought the Great Fuzzy
a big purple sack.

The Great Red Fuzzy opened it wide
And poked its head deep down inside.

"What's this?" it hollered,
and started to shout.
"There's nothing but pepper!"
and pulled back out.

"Oh, no! Oh, no! Not that!" it cried.
"A great big sneeze is building inside!"

With a great big "AAH!" and
a bigger "CHOOO!"
The Great Red Fuzzy stood up and blew!

The people were scared and
covered their eyes,
Then slowly peeked out,
and to their surprise,
Saw red fuzz all over the
ground and the trees.
It lay heaped on the streets
and blew in the breeze.

And the rest of the Fuzzy?
What happened to it?
It ran out of town,
Lickety split!

If something acts mean and bad and scary
And stomps all around and
is loud and hairy,
There may be nothing but air inside
And a very small creature trying to hide.

CPSIA information can be obtained
at www.ICGtesting.com
Printed in the USA
BVXC01n0246160614
356365BV00002B/2

9 781480 805057

written by Jeremy London
illustrated by Lonie Baranek

To Roman
JC Bank

Painted Life PUBLISHING

www.paintedlifepublishing.com

82 Plantation Pointe #2o2

Fairhope, AL 35632

At the President's house,
there's always a swirl
when welcoming leaders
from all over the world

There's a room in the house
set up just for news

Some reporters wear reds,
while others wear blues

The shoving and fighting
can even get sinister
as they welcome the visit
of India's Prime Minister

They bicker and swear
at each other with hate...

Hoping that THEIR story
won't make the news late

As the sweet gentleman
walked into the room,
all he saw were the faces
of anger and gloom.

As reporters yelled questions,
he had a bad feeling.
He put both hands together,
and looked up to the ceiling.

Then he started to giggle
and turned to his spouse.
She looked up with a smile,
as she saw a white mouse!

He fell from the sky
and into the lap
of a blue male reporter
named Barry Knapp

Then, another reporter,
a lady in red
saw the little white mouse
and darn near lost her head!

He screamed and she screamed
and they began to scatter
as secret service men asked
What's the matter?!

There's a mouse!
There's a mouse??
In the house!
In THIS house?!

There's a little white mouse?
Running loose in the house?

THERE'S A LITTLE
WHITE MOUSE
IN THIS VERY
WHITE HOUSE?!?

YES THERE'S A WHITE MOUSE
HERE IN THE WHITE HOUSE!!!!

The blues and the reds
climbed the tables in fear.
One even hung from
an old chandelier!

They hid under rugs...

... and behind statues
of Lincoln...

The sweet gentleman and his wife couldn't grasp what they're thinking

So he knelt to the floor
and scooped up in his hand
the little white mouse
that scared all those men

Then he showed all of those
at the press conference here
that a misunderstanding
is nothing to fear

He said that "A mouse is but
ONE of God's creatures,
but don't be mistaken...
It can also teach us"

That red or blue, black or white
green, brown or pink
the size of your fears
are the size that you think!

As they all looked around,
they started to laugh
at their silly response
to this funny mishap.

So, on that wild day
they were all friends again...

Thanks to a mouse...
and a sweet gentleman.

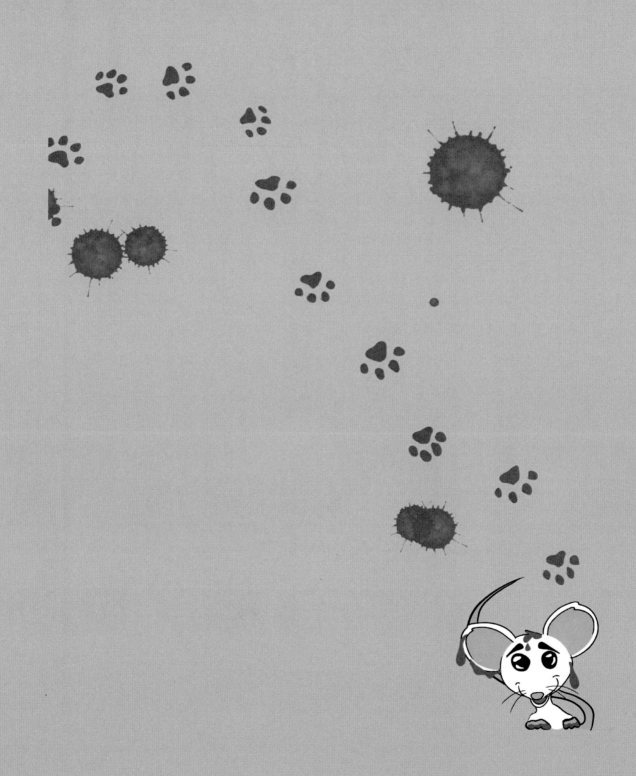

Made in the USA
Monee, IL
12 July 2020